FLE...

'...illustrated with humour and elegance on every page.'

KT-418-632

'Claude is the loveable hero of Alex T. Smith's captivating series.'

'Quirky illustrations and plenty of humour.'

'One of my favourites of the new small-format stories for beginner readers.'

'...whimsical and charming...'

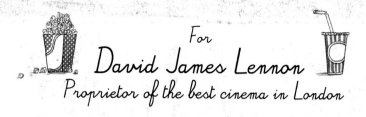

For
David James Lennon
Proprietor of the best cinema in London

A catalogue record for this book is available from the British Library

9781 444 91960 8

Design by Alison Still

Printed and bound in China

The paper and board used in this paperback by Hodder Children's Books
are natural recyclable products made from wood grown in sustainable forests.
The manufacturing processes conform to the environmental regulations of
the country of origin.

Hodder Children's Books
An imprint of Hachette Children's Group. Part of Hodder & Stoughton.
Carmelite House, 50 Victoria Embankment, London EC4Y 0DZ

An Hachette UK Company
www.hachette.co.uk

*Hodder
Children's
Books*

CLAUDE

Lights! Camera! Action!

ALEX T. SMITH

In a house on Waggy Avenue,
number 112 to be exact, there
lives a dog called CLAUDE.

Claude is a dog.
Claude is a small dog.
Claude is a small, plump dog
who wears the snazziest of
sweaters and a jaunty red beret.

jaunty red beret

snazzy sweater

Claude lives with his best friend
Sir Bobblysock who is both a sock
and quite bobbly.

He also lives with Mr and Mrs
Shinyshoes.

Every day Claude waits for them
to shout 'Cheerio!' and skip out
of the door to work, then he and
Sir Bobblysock have an adventure.

Where will our two chums go
today...?

One morning (it was a Thursday) Claude was in the garden with his beret on, and he was being VERY busy and important.

Sir Bobblysock was out there too – lying on a sun lounger with his cardigan around his shoulders.

It was the first time he'd been out of the house for a week, as he'd had a chill all down the one side.

Claude was busily and importantly hanging out all his dressing-up costumes to dry.

'There!' he said, stepping back to admire his handiwork. 'Now it is time for a treat!'

Claude whipped his beret off and had a jolly good rummage around until he found what he was looking for – a gigantic box with a trampoline inside.

It had arrived in the post the other day – a present from one of Claude's friends who had a circus.

MR BOUNCE TRAMPOLINE

Claude set up the trampoline and started to bounce.

Up and down Claude went, high up in the air. His ears flapped about beautifully behind him.

'Come and have a go!' Claude called to Sir Bobblysock.

Sir Bobblysock said that he'd love to, but he'd just had a cream horn and didn't want it coming back up again with all the bobbling about.

Claude continued to
bounce. The higher
he got, the more
he could see of
Waggy Avenue.

There
was Miss
Highkick-Spin
jazz-stepping
her way to the
dance studio.

14

And there was
Mr Lovelybuns
titivating his
buns as usual.

15

And there was a giant
gorilla in a dressing gown,
drinking a cup of tea.

A GORILLA??

IN A DRESSING GOWN??

DRINKING A CUP OF TEA??

What on earth was a giant gorilla doing on Waggy Avenue?

Claude's eyebrows started to waggle. His bottom started to wobble, and his tail began to wag so fast it was a blur.

Quickly Claude stopped bouncing and stashed the trampoline back in his beret.

'I am going to investigate this gorilla!' he cried, and ran off with Sir Bobblysock bouncing along behind him.

Unfortunately, in his excitement
to find out what was going on,
Claude managed to get his foot
caught in a dangly bit of the
washing line and –

TWAAAANNNNGGGGG! –
the whole thing fell down.

'Oh bother!' he said and quickly
stuffed all his costumes back in
his beret without even taking
them off the line.

Then Claude and Sir Bobblysock
went through the front door,
down the steps, and out into
Waggy Avenue.

23

Cor! There was ever such a lot to look at! Claude had never seen Waggy Avenue looking quite like this before.

Everywhere he and Sir Bobblysock
looked there were gigantic spotlights,
whirring cameras and big fluffy
microphones poking here, there
and everywhere.

Claude was just ogling at it all when he tripped over a bit of washing line that had escaped from his beret. Three somersaults later, he landed SMACK BANG in front of one of the waggling film cameras!

He was just thinking what a splendid landing that was – bent knees, no wobble, GORGEOUS smile – when someone shouted 'CUT!' and marched over to Claude. He looked very frowny despite the fact that he was also wearing a snazzy hat, which was currently at the jauntiest of angles.

'What are you doing!?' cried the man. 'Can't you see that we are in the middle of making a film? You just tumbled into our shot!'

Claude quickly stuffed the dangly bit of washing line back under his beret, smoothed his jumper down over his tummy and said 'sorry' in his nicest voice. This seemed to make the man with the megaphone much happier.

'It's OK,' he said, 'it was only a rehearsal. My name is Everard Zoom-Lens, and I am directing this film called *Gorilla Thriller!* It stars these two actors here – Errol Heart-Throb and Gloria Swoon.'

Claude introduced himself and Sir Bobblysock. Claude told Gloria Swoon that he liked her dangly earrings. Sir Bobblysock went a bit pink when Errol Heart-Throb shook his hand, and felt ever so glad he'd put his curlers in the night before.

'And this is our wonderful gorilla,' said Everard. 'His name is Alan.'

The enormous gorilla stood up and gave Claude and Sir Bobblysock a very dramatic bow.

He'd been classically trained.

'Would you like to watch us make our film?' asked Gloria.

Claude had never seen a film being made before so said, 'Yes please!' in his Outdoor Voice. Sir Bobblysock had seen one before, years ago, but that's a different story.

'You can sit yourself down there,' said Everard Zoom-Lens, 'and watch. There's lots for us to do before we can start filming properly.'

So Claude and Sir Bobblysock
settled themselves down and
watched closely as Errol Heart-
Throb, Gloria Swoon and the
gorilla rehearsed
their scene.

33

From what Claude could gather, the film was about a giant gorilla who had escaped from the jungle and was now hoofing up the side of a building whilst waggling Gloria Swoon about in one of his gigantic hands. Errol had to rescue her by being very handsome and brave.

It was terribly exciting.

'Right!' said Everard eventually. 'Everyone take five!'

Everyone shuffled off to their trailers to prepare for the afternoon's filming, leaving Claude and Sir Bobblysock alone.

First, Claude sat on his seat
and slurped a juice carton.
Sir Bobblysock nibbled a fig roll.

Then Claude swung his legs
for a bit and sighed.

Sitting down and waiting was
awfully boring sometimes.

Soon, Claude's eyes started
to wander...

Then his hands
wandered...

...and finally his legs followed too.

He was just sneaking back to his
seat after some terrific snooping
when a bit of the washing line
escaped from under his hat again.

'This is going to cause a terrific accident,' he said. Claude tried to stuff it back under his beret but it managed to wrap itself around one of his feet and...

Yowzer!

This time, Claude's landing wasn't anywhere near as splendid.

But at least his bottom had found something soft to bump onto...

...a

big

box of wigs!

FILM: GORILLA
THRILLER!

.WIGS.

Wigs, Claude discovered, were hairstyles that weren't attached to heads, which meant that you could try as many on as you wanted...

Claude thought he looked lovely with a full head of soft waves.

Sir Bobblysock decided to keep it all very casual.

'There you are!' said Everard Zoom-Lens. 'And you've found the wigs! Goodo! Would you be so kind as to help get them on the actors so we can start filming?'

The two chums helped the actors
put on their wigs. They did it
VERY busily and VERY
importantly.

FILM: GORILLA
THRILLER!

.WIGS.

Errol Heart-Throb had one with a kiss curl. He also had quite a ravishing fake moustache.

Gloria Swoon wore a blonde wig full of bouncy curls.

Akin had a terribly stylish toupee.

The next thing that needed to be done was make-up.

'We need them to look beautiful and very glamorous!' said Everard through his megaphone.

Claude thought faces weren't THAT different from colouring-in books. He also had some felt-tip pens, an emergency glue stick and some glitter in his beret.

As Everard dashed off to tell someone where they could put their bananas, Claude set to work...

The effect was rather striking.

'Er-lovely,' said Everard, not quite as excitedly as Claude had hoped. 'Let's get into costumes and get this film started...'

All the actors and Alan bustled off to their trailers to get changed.

55

When they emerged again, they looked like different people.

Claude clapped his paws together and Sir Bobblysock went a bit giddy at the sight of Gloria's sequins.

'Places please!' cried Everard, and everyone hurried into position. He handed Claude and Sir Bobblysock a list of jobs that needed to be done during the shoot.

The first thing was to hold
a long microphone on a
very long stick. It was
ever so heavy and
made Claude
wobble this
way and
that.

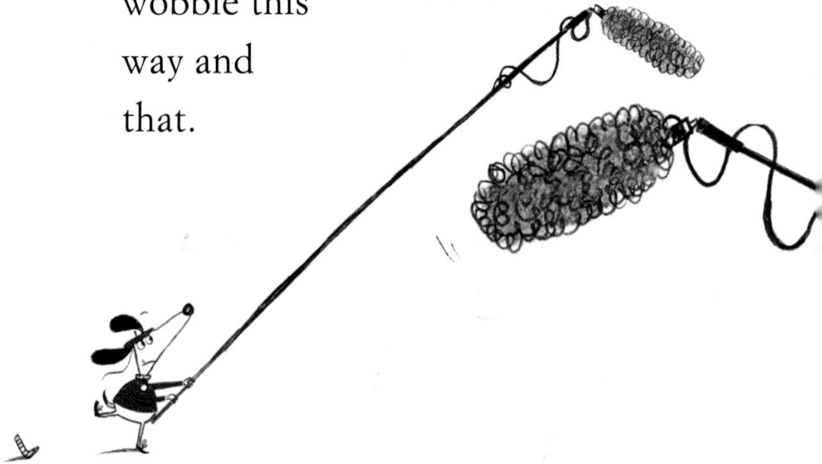

He came VERY close to walloping
a big piece of set. Luckily, Sir
Bobblysock was on hand and a
disaster was averted.

But all this meant that Claude
and Sir Bobblesock were too busy
to notice the washing line start to
snake its way out from
Claude's beret again...

The next job was to
swish a large spotlight
about so that it
followed Alan as
he swung down
Waggy Avenue.

Well, that was easier said than done – the light was so heavy Claude had to get Sir Bobblysock to help, which he did.

Everard gave the two chums a thumbs up.

Sir Bobblysock suddenly panicked. He thought he'd lost one of his contact lenses on the ground in all the excitement. Claude swung the light around for everyone to look for it. Then Sir Bobblysock remembered that he didn't actually wear contact lenses – he'd just read about someone who did in one of his magazines and got confused.

All this kerfuffle meant
  that no one noticed as a bit
    more of the washing line
      slipped out
        and started to
          dangle across
            the floor...

Soon it was time for the big end scene to be recorded – the bit where Alan had to swipe Gloria Swoon away from Errol Heart-Throb just as he was giving her a big sloppy kiss, and then shimmy up the side of Miss Melons' shop.

Claude and Sir Bobblysock dashed
back to their seats so they could
get a good view of the action.

But, in all the rush, Claude didn't
see the washing line with all his
dressing-up costumes on it slip
out from his beret *completely*.

Claude also didn't see it get
tangled around some lights,
and some cameras, and around
Gloria Swoon and Errol Heart-
Throb's feet. Lastly, it knotted
around Everard Zoom-Lens and
his megaphone...

Claude only noticed when it was too late...

Errol Heart-Throb leant in to kiss Gloria Swoon. Just as Alan the gorilla started to drag her away to scamper up the building, the washing line pulled as tight as could be and…

THUD!
CRA[S]
[C]RA[SH]
JANG[LE]

Miss Melons

Lights and
cameras tumbled
everywhere! Everard
fell on his bottom,
and Gloria Swoon and
Errol Heart-Throb went
flying across the street...

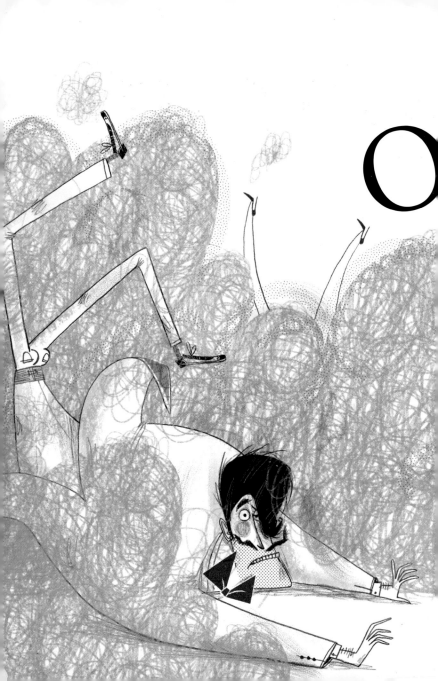

OOF!

'Uh oh...' said Claude.

Sir Bobblysock had one of his hot flushes and had to whip out his fan.

When the dust cleared, it became clear that all wasn't well.

Gloria and Errol had both twisted their ankles and had to go straight to the hospital.

As everyone dashed about to fix the mess, Everard Zoom-Lens let out a wail through his crumpled megaphone.

'Whatever will we do now?' he said. 'We can't make a film with our two lead actors in hospital! It's a disaster! If only we had two look-a-likes who could stand in for them.'

And he slumped down in a chair and went ever so limp.

Claude looked at his feet
and fiddled with the hem of
his sweater. He'd accidentally
caused this disaster with his
washing line full of dressing-up
clothes, and now he wanted to
fix it. But what could he do?

Then he had a STONKING idea!

'Me and Sir Bobblysock could
do it!'

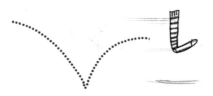

Everard smiled sadly. 'But you don't look a bit like Errol or Gloria...'

Claude smiled a hearty grin and reached into his beret.

'Just you wait!' he said.

The result was
MARVELLOUS!

'Goodness me!' cried Everard Zoom-Lens. 'You look JUST like Errol and Gloria – no one will ever know the difference! Extraordinary! Quick – let's get the cameras rolling! ACTION!'

Well, what an afternoon Claude and Sir Bobblysock had...

OH NO! I WILL SAVE YOU!

Claude shouted
his lines in his best
Outdoor Voice,
and he ran about
and lunged dramatically.

Sir Bobblysock turned out to be terribly good at fluttering his eyelashes, especially when Alan the gorilla was giving him the collywobbles.

Miss Melons'

LOVELY PEAR
Fruit and Vegetable
Emporium

And when Claude bravely rescued Sir Bobblysock and carried him safely down the ladder to the ground, everyone clapped and hooted.

After Everard had shouted
'CUT!' he trotted over to
Claude and Sir Bobblysock,
grinning from ear-to-ear.

'You were STUPENDOUS!'
he said. 'Truly wonderful!
Won't you come with us
to Hollywood and be
famous movie stars?'

But before Claude
could answer, there
came an enormous
sob from somewhere
above their heads.

It was Alan.

He was standing on top of the roof, crying and fussing with his dicky bow.

'What's the matter?'

cried Everard.

'I can't get down,' said Alan between sobs.

'Use the ladder!'

said Everard.

But Alan wouldn't.

If there was one thing he was
more frightened of than heights,
it was climbing down a ladder.

'Oh no!' said Miss Melons.
'I can't have my customers
choosing their cabbages and
picking their plums with a gigantic
gorilla crying all over them!'

She was right, of course, but Claude wondered if he could help.

Was there some way of getting Alan down that was fun and not frightening?

Of course there was!

'Come on, Alan!' cried Claude from his trampoline. 'This is a lot of fun!'

He carried on bouncing whilst Alan nervously shuffled closer to the edge.

Claude smiled his nice smile and even wagged his tail encouragingly.

At last, Alan covered his eyes,
took a deep breath and...

Miss Melons'

...leapt!

BOING!

BOING!

'A movie star AND a gorilla rescuer!' beamed Everard, joining Claude and Alan for a bounce. 'Are you sure you won't come and be a world famous actor?'

BOING!

Claude thought about it. He certainly liked dressing up and acting, but he also liked pottering about at home. And after the wigs, the sequins and being manhandled by a giant gorilla, Sir Bobblysock desperately needed one of his nice long lie-downs.

Claude explained all of this to Everard Zoom-Lens. He was disappointed, but understood.

'But you MUST keep all of the wigs!' he said, thrusting the box into Claude's paws. 'You did both look SO fetching in them.'

Claude and Sir Bobblysock thanked Everard Zoom-Lens, waved goodbye to all their new friends and went home.

Later that evening, when Mr
and Mrs Shinyshoes returned
home from work, they were
jolly surprised not only to find
a gorilla asleep in their kitchen,
but to see that both he and
Claude were wearing wigs.

'Do you think Claude knows
anything about all this?' said
Mrs Shinyshoes.

'Don't be silly!' said Mr
Shinyshoes. 'Our Claude has
been fast asleep all day...'

But Claude DID know
something about it.

And we do too,
don't we?

How to Rescue a Gorilla Should You Need To:

1 Gain their trust by complimenting them.

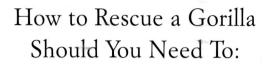

I LIKE YOUR FACE!

2 Try to persude them down by waggling a tempting banana *or two* at them.

3 Suggest they leap to safety onto the handy trampoline you keep under your hat.

MR BOUNCE TRAMPOLINE

4 If all else fails, phone the fire brigade and/or a helpful grown-up (if you know any).